The Deception

Orange Books Publication

1st Floor, Rajhans Arcade, Mall Road, Kohka, Bhilai, Chhattisgarh 490020
Website: **www.orangebooks.in**

First Edition, 2025

ISBN: 978-93-7426-230-6

Price: Rs. 299.00

Printed in India

THE DECEPTION

GULNAZ KAUR BAL

Orange Books Publication
www.orangebooks.in

Contents

Chapter - 1

The darkness has devoured the sky. As I exit my department's building, I am hit by chilling breeze that makes me shiver in my clothes while I head towards my car. Dark bellied clouds have scudded across the sky and veiled the stars in casket grey. I take a round turn and enter the line for the drive - through to stop the continuous growling in my stomach due to my late Saturday shift, which I have occasionally, during my important cases. I slide down my window to place my order, ‘‘Hi sir, what would you like to have?” A blonde probably in her teens asks me in an over-delighted voice accompanied by a wide and blinding smile, sounding too cheerful for someone working since the morning, which I am not sure she is. Well, I guess age does that to you. “Hi, I would like to have a burger with extra cheese and a medium coffee with one French fries.’’ The blonde types away on her tablet frantically while her pony moves to and fro slightly, ‘‘You’ll have your order within 5 to 7 minutes, while you can pay your bill on the machine ahead.” I nod my head and head towards the machine where my name is already displayed with the bill amount. I pay my bill through my card, and after receiving my order, again join the highway connected to the route to my apartment while enjoying my meal. I can only see spotless white and yellow dots indicating cars. It is 8 pm, which is not my usual time for a Saturday, as I head for home early. As a 32 - year- old I get exhausted really fast while solving minor cases which do not need any special investigation. I think my job as a police officer has eaten away the last few brain cells and energy that I have left with. Finally, after precisely half an hour of reckless driving, I reach my apartment and park my car. Each apartment has an adequate parking area to park a car belonging to the residents. This building does not exactly give rich people vibes, but yeah reflects the look that people living in it are having enough money to live freely. The view from my flat is quite beautiful as it faces most of the city. I unlock the door by entering the passcode, which even a 2 - year - old child can crack without knowing any counting. I enter my apartment and am instantly met with the sight of spilt milk across my kitchen counter. "What the fuck, whoever has entered my apartment needs to come out right now because whoever has come to my apartment has made a big fucking mistake…" "Cool down, bro, you need to calm yourself and get your shit together," I recognise the voice of my best friend immediately, and a sigh of relaxation leaves my body. His hands are crossed over his chest, and his one leg is slanting, and the other leg crosses over the slanting leg while he leans against the wall, wearing a large shirt of black and white strips that could contain two of him and a simple pair of trousers. "How the hell do you expect me to calm down when I know that some stranger has entered my apartment and is still probably here?" A flash of feeling passes his face which I cannot decipher, and sudden relaxation dawns upon me. "Did you..."

"Yes, I did, but before you try to beat the shit out of me for scaring you to death, it is not my fault that I entered when I needed some milk to make a latte for me when you have disgrace for a password." "So, you figured my password out?" He lifts one eyebrow as he directs a look of sarcasm towards me. Okay, now I definitely need to change my password. "Stan, I think you need to sleep, bro, otherwise you have the capability of giving a poor old hag a heart attack." "What are you saying?" I step in front of the mirror in the corridor. My house cannot be called precisely big, but it has decent space, and most of all, it is my home and my paradise for me. Adjacent to the door is the kitchen and further down the corridor are 2 bedrooms with attached washrooms and in between the kitchen and the bedrooms. I have a mini drawing room with two small paintings hung on the wall to adorn and make it seem homey with a balcony sufficient to nurture a few plants, not that I do. When I look at the mirror, I almost don't recognise myself, I look at least 5-6 years older than I am with my wrinkled shirt, mushed up hair and two black holes for my dull and red - looking eyes and pale skin. "Shit, man." "Yes, bro, you look like shit, and yes, I am leaving as you need to sleep and give yourself some much - needed sleep." After he leaves, I lock the door after changing the password from 1234 to 0987. Yes, I know, it was 1234. Without bothering to change, I straight away go to my room and fall on the bed, and within 1 minute darkness surrounds me as I drift off to sleep.

Chapter - 2

Curtains of white piercing through my window make my eyes shrink, keeping my hand in front of my eyes I try to block out the light. The alarm on my bedside table begins to ring, to notify me that it is time to go for my morning 8 am walk with my best friend Randy. Well, his full name is Randell Shelley, but for me it is Randy, and for him my name is Stan, not Sterlley Rampant. I am a guy with a tough physique standing 6 feet 2 inches of height, but the guy towers over me with his 6 feet 4 inches and a robust body adorned with a soft core inside. By soft core inside, I mean the guy cannot put a rein on his feelings, which is why he is working as a coder in a big company as an app developer and not as a police officer while I am just like how I am on the inside, tough. I do not connect with any of the cases emotionally, just mentally. One thing which I praise myself unconditionally for is that I do not mess my personal life with my professional life. Not bragging, but I am one of the best police officers in the department, which is not in any way helping me to get interesting and mysterious cases. I can't remember even if I ponder the days when I got an interesting case. I tap the alarm to switch it off and get changed into my sports clothes, which has a2 look close to a night suit with its full black colour, loose and informal as hell look. I wear my Nike sports shoes, brush my teeth and wash my face, and within 5 minutes join in with Randy, who is, as usual, waiting for me in the corridor. His house is just adjacent to mine, which gives me comfort sometimes and hassle the other times, depending upon the situation. He is wearing his usual pyjama with a plain blue shirt, completely in contrast to his blinding white Puma shoes. "Hey bro, if you need today's Sunday off for resting, I really don't mind. Anyway, you're going to run less and crawl like a snail more, which is completely in contrast to my lethal speed while running," he says with almost a proud smile. "Shut it, and move," I say with a frustrated note in my voice. "Okay, I get it, you are not used to people telling you that you look like shit and making you do things on their terms, which is happening quite a lot these days. But I need you to be alright, you are my only family left." This renders me speechless. Randy had been in foster care for 6 years, moving from one place to another every 6 months, when he lost his parents at the tender age of 12 years in a brutal car accident. On his birthday, when he attained the age of 18, he applied internships at various cities and got selected almost everywhere. He accepted the internship from New York, where we became roommates as we were not in a state to pay individual rent, as I had sworn not to take a penny from my parents, who are well - known architects. He worked his ass off for many years and went from working for a small company to a huge ass company, while I did away with my police training. We both skipped our college years, me to get out of my parents' toxic environment, and him as he didn’t want to experience more of people’s pretension of showing love just to get the government’s compensation for raising an orphan. He did not like to be reminded of his childhood and did not talk about it, but now I could see the dwelling feeling of agitation and fear of losing his only family left. His bobbing throat and wet, scrutinizing eyes looked at me to register my response and reply. "I will be alright, I promise," I say with sternness in my voice and sounding completely different. He gazes at me for 5-6 seconds and nods. We run on like maniacs to let all our emotions off and return within 1.5 hours and go to our own apartments to take a bath and freshen up. Before I can take off my clothes, the ring of continuous sms renders me curious. I pick up my mobile and open the sms and look at the pieces of articles, blurred photos and newspaper headlines. Shit, the messenger of Jesus has been crucified and just like old times, darkness shall conquer and rule.

Chapter - 3

I wake up to the screeching sound of my alarm and get changed into my uniform after freshening up and breakfast. I take the lift to go to the ground floor, as I live on the fifth floor and get in my car. I drive for around 35 minutes while listening to songs on full volume and enjoying my early morning drive. I am not an early bird, but since I have to wake up at 6 am in the morning, then why not enjoy the sound - free environment and the sight of nature? To someone else it might be a normal scene, but for me the beauty of nature is enhanced while its beauty is not neglected, underestimated and remains undisturbed from human interventions. In the morning, a new hope rises with the sun to shine and spread brightness around the world. For me, every day is a new start that could give me unexpected and endless opportunities to prove myself to the world that doesn't believe in me. I reach my department's building and, after parking my car, head off to my office. Just as I enter and start to go off to my office, a voice that I adore with all my heart stops me in my tracks. Laurence Northman, who is also the police commissioner of New York and the closest father figure that I have while my real father is alive, had given me all the support which I needed when I was new here and still doing my police training. He cannot be called a handsome man, but has decent features for a 63 -year- old man with a slim nose, puffed up lips, almond - shaped brown eyes, with his white complexion, which could also be mistaken for pale skin. “I would need you in my office within 5 minutes,” he says without displaying any emotions and accompanied by a sternness that I am not accustomed to. “Yes, sir,” I say while saluting. Everyone looks at me as if expecting me to say something, and after registering my lack of response, everyone resumes their work. I don’t blame them, our commissioner hardly comes out of the confined space of his office, and if he does then either it could be a matter of eternal joy or a matter of utmost concern. I knock on his door “May I come in, sir?” I wait for his response and enter as I hear a fragile ‘yes.’ He beckoned me over to sit in front of him on the black chair opposite his chair with a brown table in the middle, which was messed up with different old files, pens, pencils and old pictures of numerous cases. Laurence Northman was a man known for his cleanliness, and some even called him a freak. “You must be wondering why I called you here. I want you to scramble through a link that I have sent you now, just a few moments earlier.” He gestures for me to open the link. Within one second of tapping on the link, I am met with the astonishing and familiar photos in front of me. The Pope. “What about it?” I say with a completely clueless voice, even though I know where this conversation is headed. “I won’t beat around the bush and cut straight to the chase. I want you to take charge of the case.” He says without an ounce of hesitation. “Why me?” “Because, as far as I have known you, you have been a determined and hardworking person, which is also the kind of attitude needed to solve this case. Moreover, I know that you haven't been honoured with a case to keep your brain on the run since I don't know how long."

"Sir, I appreciate your concern, but I don't want to be known as the man whose career was handed down to him just because he had the sympathy of an old man to keep his career running." I love Lauren as a father figure and as a friend, but I wouldn't want anyone to do any unnecessary favours for me that could put me in debt, which I would have to pay later at the expense of something valuable. I trust him not to do something like that to me, but human nature is the most unpredictable one, and time can put you in a spot where you might have to do something that you don't want to, especially with a job like this. He smiles and says, "I knew you would come up with an argument like this, but I just want to clear that neither do I differentiate nor do I have a better choice than you." Your unyielding determination could be of great use in this case. I am not handing you over your career, but I am just providing you with an opportunity to prove yourself and your worth not only to the people who don't care whether you exist or not but also to yourself and extract the old enthusiastic and excited Sterlley Rampant who loved being a police officer back to life. I am merely a means, but it is still you who has to solve the case and prove to the world his unyielding faith in himself." His words are like a jab to my heart, which straightaway passes through it and makes me realise the grave mistake I was on the verge of committing, which could later on cost me my future in the name of my self - esteem. “When should I begin?” His eyes shrink at the ends while he tries to put a reign on his ready to be on display smile. “Today, if you deem it comfortable and convenient. Just keep in mind that this case is none like the other; it involves people’s religious sentiments that you could invoke without even intending. So, deal with it carefully and do not say something under the exhort of the media that you might later on regret.” I nod, giving him a brisk salute and walk out the door with completely distinguished emotions as when I was entering. Without the matter of 15 minutes, I have been handed over the case that I had received continuous sms about and which has gained national attention. Looks like we have a killer to catch.

Chapter - 4

I straightaway head towards the Church in the corner of the valley of marshes street after Laurence forwarded me the full address of the church. I did some digging into the church that could give me a background, and came up with some information that even a commoner would know, and some information about the person who built it. It was built in 1980 by a very conservative and religious person who was loaded with money. Unlike other affluent people, he was known to be a man of the kindest of hearts and a positive attitude towards helping people. His name was Credy Myre, who came from a very average- earning family and thus was exposed to the hardships faced by a common man. He worked unceasingly to attain the level of success that he had and built the church for serving to serve the public, as he believed that the biggest support that he could offer was God's grace upon the people and provide them a place to share their happiness and sorrow. Unfortunately, his and his family’s death was sudden, and the reason is unknown to date. I reach the church and get out of my police vehicle. I am met by throngs of people stopped by the yellow ribbon tied from one point of the door to the other, indicating a crime scene. The people at least have the decency to part the way leading to the entry of the church. As I enter, I notice that the church is just like other churches with a portrait of Mother Mary and Saint Joseph hung on either side of the nave, in front is the crucified statue of Jesus surrounded by a police officer, a priest and a few nuns. As I reach the statue, the police officer who seems a few years younger than me shoots me a salute and tells me his name, but I am too struck by the sight in front of me to pay any heed to any of the people present there. The Pope is lying dead on the stairs leading to the statue of Jesus. The Pope's eyes are closed, and there is an imprint of enclosed fingers around his throat, indicating strangulation and no signs of blood. "Sorry, could you repeat your name and tell me all the information about the pope which you've gained?" The officer whose name is apparently John Bryce, without wasting a minute, pours all the information that he has, which is close to nothing, for which I don't blame him. As much data as I have collected, I came to know that he was a very socially inactive person who used to keep to himself, but was always present in all the religious gatherings, and his name was Dean Lopez. No one is aware of his history, which is justified as he did not like to mingle unnecessarily with anyone. "When is the forensic team arriving?" "I have already informed them, and they could be arriving any minute now." Okay, so apparently my assigned partner isn't completely useless. I nod, "Did they use to work with the pope?" I say while gesturing towards the priest and nuns. Yes, sir, apparently, they were one of the few people he was on talking terms with or was maybe compelled to talk to due to their working at the same place." "I'll go and talk to them." "As you wish, sir." I head towards them while their heads swirl towards me, and all the nuns except one and the priest leave. The priest has a minor mark on his hand, which is negligible if not paid attention to. Their faces are not displaying any emotion, but I can point to a flicker of pain latched onto the nun's face, which is almost negligible if you don't pay any special attention to it, while the priest's face is hard to comprehend. "I am sorry to have to disturb you on an unfortunate incident like this, but I have to shower you with a few questions. It would be appreciated if you could cooperate for the few upcoming minutes." "We would be obliged to offer any kind of help that could lead you to the potential killer." The priest says solemnly. "I appreciate that, so how long had you known Father?" The nun speaks up this time. "We had known him for 6 years as we both began to work at almost the same time." I jot down each and every detail that I am getting in the register that I opened while asking the question. "Was he originally from here or had he come here from some other place? How was he nature - wise? Did he have any disputes with anyone regarding anything in the past?" "His nature was the farthest from a violent person, and even if he did not agree with someone, he would express his disagreement without resignation. He was a very reserved person and happily accepted and enjoyed his seclusion from the world. He loved his own company, and as much as we would have loved to tell you but we are not aware of his real native place. We talked, but only regarding various events and work and did not take our conversations to the extent of our personal lives." The priest answered. "Did you experience something abnormal about his behaviour in recent days?" "No, he was completely normal." The priest says with a grim expression. "Can you give me the address of his residence?" Despite not being a religious person, I am aware that a pope is to stay in the Apostolic Palace in Vatican City, but I just don't want to leave anything unturned. "Yes, we can give you his address." "Yes, please." The priest hands me the address on a piece of paper. His handwriting is sleek and as clear as if written on an electronic device. "I would like to ask my last question: where and when did you see him the last time?" Since it is already 9 am in the morning, I am guessing they saw him last yesterday. "The church closes at 6 pm, so when I was leaving at around 5:30 pm-6 pm for the convent at the far back end of the church when I last saw him." "I left a little late, as yesterday we had a mass, and I had to listen to the Sacrament of Penance. I left at exactly 6:30 pm, and last saw him then in the church only. He used to leave later after completion of his Divine office." "Didn't you have to do your night prayer?" "I was headed to my rectory for my night prayer" "I also did my night prayer at the convent after leaving the church," the nun speaks up. I scribble down every ounce of information I am getting. "Thank you for your cooperation, and I would reach out to you if I need any more specifications in relation to something." "We would be glad to assist you if we are capable." The priest says. During the interview, I did not get a glimpse of impatience, which is new as people mostly give went to their feelings, but again they have been trained to get a grip of their emotions even in times like this. The name of the priest was

Stenhart Wagganor, and the nun's name was Nancy Claize, as John told me. “I want no one to enter and the church to be sealed for a few days. The forensics report should be on my table within 48 hours and convey to the team that this is an emergency and a sensitive case, so act after putting a veil on even the minor details. No word should get out regarding the case, and I want you to dig out information on any of the family members of the deceased, whether dead or alive.” “Yes, sir, what should we do with the media?” “Fucking media, always ready to escalate an issue to raise their freaking TRPs, do not provide them with any real information, just beat around the bush and dismiss them.” I say with a frustrated growl. I am not concerned about the nun and the priest leaking the information, as I know they must be bound by their morals or whatever to do something like that. I somehow managed to pass the crowd gathered without stumbling and being pushed over. The people have started to make their own theories, and the murmuring and whispers are really getting to me. I briskly walk towards the police vehicle I came in with the longest strides I can take without seeming to be in a hurry. The media have not followed me around, which means that they probably have got the message that they won't be getting the big catch they were hoping for from this case. As a police officer my biggest enemy is not the culprit but the people who give all the lead to the people around the globe which we have sacrificed countless sleep for just so that they can cook up their own ridiculously close to impossible theories and criticise us for not giving the result in

2-3 days when the actual worth of time is most well-known to us. Among the people who receive the news can also be the culprit who could take precautionary measures by keeping an eye on our every move through the media and always be 4 steps ahead of us. I get in the car and within 30 minutes reach the commissioner's office and give a report on all the information I have gathered. "Sir, do you really think that I need another officer to work with me to resolve the case?" I say with a certain level of hesitation. "I am not by any means skeptical about your capabilities but John is just a few years younger than you and whether you want his assistance or not is totally dependent on you but he would be staying under your wing so that he gets exposed to the way cases are to be handled whether you like it or not, if there are no more question you can leave officer." He says with a dismissive and authoritative tone. "Yes, sir." I walk out the door and keep in mind not to disturb him due to his not - so - good mood, which is not frequent. After reaching home, I open my laptop and run a search for Dean Lopez and come up with nothing but the name of the church where he worked. Weird.

Chapter - 5

The next day I wake up and follow the same routine but with a speed I did not know I possessed as I was awakened by the frantic ringing of my phone and greeted by a voice which I was getting accustomed to. John told me that the forensic report had arrived, and Lucy Harding, who was a member of the forensic team, only had 2 hours to spare and provide me with the details of the case. I enter my office and see John sitting inside beside a woman of fair but not too white complexion, she seems to be in her late 20s. John stands up and salutes me while I nod and shake hands with Lucy. Her grip is as firm as mine as she greets me, “Good morning, officer.” She says with a soothing yet stern voice. “Good morning, Miss Lucy, it is a pleasure. I hope I did not keep you waiting for long.” “No, I just arrived a few minutes earlier, and I should be apologetic to call you before your office hours.” She says with an apologetic smile, marries her face. “There is no fixed time for the work of the police miss,” I say with a hint of sarcasm and smile. “Let’s begin, shall we? Now, as you might know that the reason for death is manual strangulation. There are obviously signs of asphyxia in addition to purple bruising on the neck of 1-2 cm in size. Minor scratches are marinating the victim's body, indicating resistance. There is also bleeding from the larynx, which occurs when excessive force is applied to cut the circulation of air. During the autopsy, we found scrapings from under the fingernails of the deceased, which gives us the blood group of the culprit but there are no finger prints on the neck which is only feasible to occur if the person committing to this crime has covered his bare hands by some kind of glove or covering to prevent the hand imprint on the neck of the victim. The DNA report would require one more day to be released. Till the time I can provide you with the reports so you can study them in brief, and by tomorrow I can provide you with the DNA report." "Very well then, please do forward me the DNA report as soon as it arrives." "Yes, officer, will do." She says politely and, after providing me with the report, makes a move towards the door. After she leaves, I look at John, whom I had close to forgotten was seated there. He is so lost in thought that even if someone shot a bullet, he won't give a damn. He seems completely oblivious to his surroundings. I have to make a sound by my throat two times to make him recollect himself from his anonymous thoughts and grab his attention. Even if he got frustrated by me interrupting his thoughts, he does a good job at hiding it. "I told you to gather information about the family members of Dean Lopez. Did you find something of value?" "Yes, sir, apparently the pope was an orphan whose parents had committed suicide when he was 16 years old. He took over as the pope when Cryde Myre and his family died mysteriously, as he had no parents, he wanted to devote himself to God and wanted to separate himself from the world of pretensions. He was originally from Washington, DC, but none of his family members are known to be alive." Since none of his family members were alive, we have to go to the place where it all started. "Pack your bag, John, looks like we are going to Washington."

Chapter - 6

The drive from New York to Washington is of 226 miles which takes us several hours. I had been granted to leave New York for the investigation by the police commissioner, along with John. John told me the address of the place where the pope used to live in his childhood. We reach our destination and are met with the sight of consecutive brick houses adjourned to each other, of rusting brown colour and separated by a close - to - negligible thin fence. It is at that moment that I am hit with a putrid smell. I turn and notice that a woman was frying eggs in a pan with her kitchen window open. John looks like he has also noticed the same. “Did not expect the pope to have come from such a poor background.” He says with a grim expression. I nod, “Let’s get over with the work that we are here for, lead the way, John.” He ushers me to a house that seems to be on the verge of falling down any minute, with a compact space that could at most contain 4 members. We enter the house and are attacked by a rotten and rusty smell that makes me want to puke, but I somehow restrain the need to get the hell out of the house as soon as possible. And looking at John's expressions, he doesn’t follow some other emotions, his one hand is covering his nose with a handkerchief. We enter one of the rooms where everything remains scattered, indicating that no one has made the effort to make the place look decent. Not that I blame them for not giving a care in the world for the house where two people had committed suicide. There is one cushion which is placed in the corner of the rooms, while there is a portrait hung on a wall that is hidden behind a thick layer of dust. I wipe the dust off with my handkerchief. The first thing I notice is the twinkling eyes of a toddler and a five to seven - year - old child standing beside two women and two men. What pushes me to the far end in the corner of my mind is the cross cutting the face of the elder child. I touch the cross and feel the engraved sign on the tips of my fingers. I withdraw my hand and direct my attention towards the other people. One man is wearing an expensive as hell suit while the other is wearing a mediocre one, they are gazing at the camera with a full eye stretching grin that marries their faces. Besides the men, there are two women whose dresses are like the men's, in complete contrast with each other. The woman who is carrying the toddler in her arms is graced by a jewel that people would kill for, and the child completely resembles her slender almond shaped eyes and full, plump lips, while his body seems to have taken after his father, who is obviously the man wearing the expensive suit. The toddler is wearing the same - coloured clothes in complete coordination with his father’s. “Who could’ve made the cross on the face of the child?” John utters with a contemplative expression while examining the picture. “The million - dollar question is, who are the people standing next to the pope’s family? Looking at the picture, it is close to impossible that they could be family. Their features, their style of dressing and the cost of the clothes they are wearing make it a slim chance. But at the same time, destiny is a bitch, it has the power to provide you with lifelong treasures and to also make you beg for a grain." I say, while my thoughts are running so fast, they could beat a metro, inspecting all the directions and methods that could provide us with the answers to a few questions that are currently eating away at my brain. "Let's question the neighbour, if not much, they would know the lifestyle of the family," John says with a typical, ready - to - question voice of a police officer. I nod, and as I start to leave, in the corner of my eye, I catch a glint of something peaking from behind the dressing table below the portrait. I ask for a glove from John, who stops his stealthy pace and turns his gaze to where I am looking. He wastes no time and hands me a glove after fetching it from the car. I moved the dresser with John's assistance. A sudden squeaky sound greets me, and a mouse emerges from the back of the dresser and runs from the gap between my feet. I look at the back, and the dust accumulated in the back makes it even harder to notice. I grasp it and shove away all the dust hindering the visibility of the note. It is written in very clear handwriting as if written by someone who had attended writing classes. John and I share a secret look of communication with our eyes.

“Looks like we’ve got a lead.”

Chapter - 7

Dear 4514121516526

I was completely intrigued to know you from the moment I became aware of my surroundings. You always made me want to be like you. The more I grew up, the more I idolised you, not only me, but my family thought so highly of you and your family. As a child, I even saved my pocket money to buy you gifts on your birthday, which was a great sacrifice from a child who was frugal as hell with it. I guess that no one has the right to be idolised because no human deserves to be, we are not perfect, no one is. It just depends upon the ability of the person to hide behind the cloak of his good deeds and manoeuvre his wrongdoings in such a pit that it can not crawl up. I thought you proved me wrong and shielded me like a big brother that I never had. Unfortunately, I was wrong. We humans, have a tendency to work for something only if driven by the temptation of reward. You were no different. You were worse than a cobra that at least raises their fangs before biting. You engraved your close - to - perfect image in our eyes in such a way that it was all that was visible. I was living in delusion until I was assaulted by the reality that made me feel like I was standing on a cliff and was pushed over by the hand that would be there to save me. The nightmares still catch me in the middle of the night, my mind is still plagued by the horrifying yells, the lifeless eyes and the dripping of blood. The days of peace are gone because I will fulfil my dream of fantasies of killing you slowly and steadily and wreak havoc on your life such that your trembling soul wishes we never crossed paths. You took something invaluable from my life, and it is only fair I return the favour. Pray as much as you can because God might forgive you, provide you redemption from your deeds, and spare you from being shoved in the dark pits of hell, but my salvation won't be until I rip your soul out and pulverize it. I am coming for you. Big brother.

Chapter - 8

John and I haven't recovered from the aftershocks of letter we just read. Who the hell is thc big brothcr and the younger brother, and why can't criminals do straight crimes and head off? Why leave clues like writing a number for a name? Who does that? There is a connection between the letter and the pope, given that it is from his home, we just have to figure out what. What is more concerning is that this shit takes time and patience, which in my case is ticking off as the media spreads countless pathetic strategies to the public who feed it off like dogs starved for one to two weeks have been handed over a bowl full of bones while they breathe down our neck. It is a Homicide case, not a toy got stolen now find the thief case for fuck's sake, that they want instant results. After thoroughly searching the house, we came up with nothing but a few dead mice and insects that I have encountered for the first time and dirt that had the potential to hide a dead body inside it. John has taken a photo of the portrait hung in the house just in case we require it anytime in New York. He is driving while my whole attention is dwelling on the scenarios that could have prospered. "What do you think of the letter? Who could have written it?" I say to end the deafening silence clawing at my chest. "I am as much in thought as you sir; there are numerous possibilities. I just don't want to dwell on them till the time we don't get the real hint to direct our thoughts towards a particular direction. Otherwise, we might travel down the wrong road and never reach the destination." He looks at me for a second and says, "It's dark, so let's head towards the hotel that I booked, unless we want the darkness to devour us like insects on a corpse now, shall we, sir?"

Chapter - 9

We stayed the night in a 3 star hotel which is not bad considering the place we just had paid a visit to. The rooms were comfortable with their king - sized beds and with profuse eating and drinking items in the fridge. After taking a hot bath and eating to my fullest, and shut down my thoughts as exhaustion - induced sleep overtakes me. The next day, I wake up and join John, who is sitting in the buffet and furiously typing away at his phone with such force that it would be no surprise if his phone's screen cracked. I approach him, and his attention snaps as he looks at me and keeps his phone on the side, his features barely restraining his emotions. He is wearing an irritable expression and tries to school it as soon as he sees me approaching, but in vain. With a plate filled with different types of cuisines I had no idea existed, I sat down opposite John, who displayed the non - required decency of waiting for me to arrive to dig in, which filled me with a kind of guilt that had no place being there. “You didn’t have to wait for me,” I say with a neutral expression. “It is okay, sir, I was only here five to ten minutes before you, so it isn’t like you kept me waiting long anyway,” John said. “Well, now that I have arrived, let’s dig in.” We eat our food with no haste and devour each chunk. The first bite of lasagna fills me with a feeling of contentment as my mouth gets loaded by the rich flavour of cheese, meat sauce and blocks of chicken. After precisely half an hour, we have eaten and start driving towards the Pope's house. As we reach, we are met with the familiar sight of what we witnessed yesterday. The people in groups are chit - chatting, and the women are carrying vegetables they must have just bought while bickering to each other. We head towards a group of women who look at us with curiosity. “Good morning, ma’am, I am Sterlley Rampant and and this is John Bryce, my partner. We are from the New York police department of homicide and wanted to enquire you regarding the family that resided in that house.” I say that while pointing towards the house of the Pope. The ladies look at me like I have sprouted another head and while shooting me an apologetic glance, say, “Sorry, but we don’t think we can be of any use to you." They disperse, but a woman stops in her tracks and half turns towards me, "You should go to Saunders Laurson, who lives just around the corner of the street." She resumes walking towards the other women. John and I walk towards the house in the corner of the street that seems not too far away. From a distance we see a house whose walls have been eaten away by termites, and the plants are all dead due to a lack of water. As we close to the house, a different kind of energy I can't place grips me. The house seems to have had less movement in it than a grave at 12 at midnight. Just as John is going to knock, a pair of dim eyes peeping through a window on the opposite side of the same wall catches me off guard. The eyes display no emotion. She moves from the window, and suddenly the door opens with a low creaking sound as a woman in her late eighties greets us. She looks fragile, and her face is a crisscross of wrinkles. Her eyes are black in colour with wrinkles at the end, indicating her age. She is slightly bent, and her attire is of a woman living in deep poverty. “Won’t you come in? You surely have a lot to talk about.” She says with a faint smile as if she knew we would reach out one day.

Chapter - 10

We sit in awkward silence for what seems to be an eternity while the old woman whose name is apparently Saunder Laurson, moves at a pace that seems she is moving in slow motion. Again, not her fault. She asks while standing, "Do you want tea?" She says with a genuine expression. "No, thank you." She seems to be a genuine person, but after noticing her slow-as-a-snail pace, I don't want to drain out my time and also not trouble her. She nods and takes a seat opposite me while John is seated adjacent to me. "May we ask you a few questions, ma'am?" Obviously, she has allowed her inside her house because she is okay with that, but a man doesn't have to let go of basic decency while talking to an elderly person. She nods. "Did you know Dean Lopez and his family? Does his name ring a bell?" I ask, trying to restrain the hope from leaking into my voice and miserably failing. "Yes, I did. They were my best friends once." She says with an expression that resembles a person who has been hit by reality and a quivering voice. "What does once mean?" John asks. Her expression remains the same while she says, "No, we were inseparable before they met them." Her calm expression wavers a little. "Who met whom?" She looks at me with a thunderous expression that seems to have overcome the calm one. "They were so relentless in their pretensions, trying to stay always in the spotlight and pretend to be of the kindest of hearts, always assisting those in need, while behind all these kind actions was a person afraid to show his true self, a monster lurking in the dark and ready to feed upon the darkness." With each passing line, her voice seems to have risen a thousand notches and attained a level which I deemed her unworthy of achieving. Her eyes are bulging out, and she starts coughing hard. "Ma'am, you okay?" She starts shaking vigorously and breathes in and out hard. We stand and rush towards her, "Call an ambulance." I yell at John, who is already on the phone calling for an emergency ambulance. "G..go to the h..house of Cryde M..myre. His death.." Her lips stop moving as I watch her life leave her body.

Chapter - 11

After the ambulance arrived, Saunder's body was taken away for autopsy just in case. While I was stressing myself by pondering about what she said to dying. Cryde Myre's house, but why? There must be a connection, but what? How are the two families bonded? I was told that even his family, including him, was murdered, the pope's parents also committed suicide, and he was also murdered. Is there an invisible thread tying these cases? Why was the old woman taking their name with such rage, and if she knew what, why did she not inform the police concerned with the case at the time? I am thoroughly aware that the case of Cryde Myre was investigated when it occurred, but no clues concerning the culprit were found. John, who is sitting in the driver's seat, is inquiring regarding Cryde Myre's house on his phone. "Okay, thank you." He keeps his phone down and says, "Cryde Myre's house is close by. He lived in the elite street of Washington, which is just a few miles away." Wait, if he lived in Washington, too, then why was the church built in New York? "I am not able to think with a clear head, why would he build the church in New York rather than in Washington if it was more convenient?" John says, as if he just read my mind and displayed my thoughts out in the open. We look at each other just at the same time and instantly realise we are thinking the same, there is definitely a connection between the two cases of Cryde Myre and the pope.

Chapter - 12

We reach Cryde Myre's house in about two hours. Guess when John said a few miles, it was an understatement. The house is situated in a street whose sights are to behold. The street, the houses and every single thing enclosed in this elite street can send a dying man into ecstasy. It is such a sight. While on our way here, we discovered two massive parks, one for the elders for a walk and the other for children with different kinds of swings and slides that are every child's dream at an age. The parks were equally maintained with the same kind of layout and adorned with different kinds of bushes and marshes cut in different shapes like circles, squares etc, while the elders park had a simple yet elegant and tranquil look. The people here were so overly dressed up they looked straight out of Oscars, even while on a walk with their dogs. I saw a person whose dog was wearing a coat with an intricate design, and by the look of it, it was expensive. It was probably more than a normal person's monthly income, for Christ's sake. And saying these were houses was the biggest understatement that I could have delivered. These were not houses, these were freaking bungalows with a massive garden in the front and the back. A look at John told me he was thinking the same; he looked astonished. "When I was told he was wealthy, I did not expect this. This place is fucking majestic." I look at John, he must be really startled if he used the f word, which is way out of his always disciplined character. We get out of our car after parking it on the side of the road. If my occupation were not police, I would be a little anxious about people calling the police upon us, but since our car is a cop car itself, no one would express their discomfort anytime soon. Not that I like to create discomfort, but a man tends to take advantage of something if given a chance. By the looks of the lifestyle these people are used to, they are not accustomed to discomfort and would not wait for more than a few hours to report on us, even if we are the police themselves. The afternoon weather is oppressive. We take a few steps on the pavement till we are greeted by the massive black painted gates marking the entrance of the house.

Sorry, bungalow. We open the gate, which in turn creates a creaking sound unpleasant to the ears. We enter the bungalow through the main gate, and our nostrils are instantly filled with dust. We wave our hands to clear the air around us while coughing. The bungalow is not in a bad but a miserable state. Straight ahead are stairs that lead up and diverge towards two sides, which I assume contain rooms. The place where the stairs diverge hangs a painting of two children. One is a toddler, while the other is a child of around five to six years of age. It contains the same toddler in the portrait I saw at the Pope's house, it means the toddler is Myra’s son. I take a snap of the painting on my phone and ascend the stairs, first heading towards the right side. I open the first door, and suddenly a screeching sound greets me, and a bat exits the room from above my head. I bend on instinct. The room is dark and barely. I open the curtains and discover spider webs in almost every corner of the room. After going through the room, I head over to the next room. The next hour goes by in futile searching. I enter the last room with the expectation of coming out empty - handed. While searching the room, I look into a drawer and find nothing. After releasing a sigh I look around the room, and my gaze snaps to a heavily heaving John standing at the entrance with a pair of gloves in a plastic. "Wasn't the pope murdered with a glove sort of covering?"

Chapter - 13

We are sitting in the car while dead silence surrounds us. My thoughts are running like they are in a freaking marathon. The glove must have got here after the investigation of the house was completed; there is no chance the police would have left anything which might have been of even a little use. But it also leaves us with a time span of more years we can envision ourselves inquiring about. The glove could be anyone's; it doesn't need to be the pair with whom the murder was interlinked. But if it is, why is it here? It definitely cannot be a coincidence. I have given a clear order to retrieve the camera footage of the church on the day of the murder, but I am positive it would provide no lead, no murderer would be foolish enough to not know where the cameras are fixed while planning to murder someone. The whole house was clear, and we found nothing except the pair of gloves. But why would the old lady take his name before dying if they were not connected? Surely, she knew something, but only if we knew what. My phone starts ringing, startling both of us. I reach into my pocket and pick up the call. "Hello," I say. "Good evening, sir, I wanted to inform you that we have received the blood report and retrieved the camera's footage." An unrecognised voice informs me. "Okay, keep it safe, I'll have a look when I return."

"Okay, sir."

"Did anyone have a look at it?"

"No, sir." Great, I don't need anyone to add to my worries. Technology can be taken advantage of and used to present the data the way you want. I don't fucking trust it, and after all, it has been designed by humans, who are even less trustworthy than animals. I hang up and inform John the same. "Let's get down and inquire about Cryde Myre, he would have been in his sixties, so we could get a hold of some of his acquaintances in the neighbourhood if they still live here." "Okay, sir" John nods, and we both get down of the car. We go and ring the bell of the house parallel to the house we investigated. This house is precisely of the same size with a massive black coloured gate shaped in quite intricate designs in the front. An old woman, seemingly in her seventies, greets us. She has wrinkles and is dressed up, not in the clothes I would buy to go to the Oscars, she is heavily loaded with souvenirs that must have cost a fortune. She is wearing a black gown with cleavage meant to be seen, and the black gown has golden colored design on it. It must be heavy as hell. She looks at us with an astonished expression. I am well acquainted with the expression, some people make it due to fear, some people due to shock, some due to being frightened and some due to confusion. “How can I help you?” She asks with a little, fragile and bored voice.

Chapter - 14

"Good evening ma'am, we just wanted to inquire about a case, if you could just give us a few minutes." The lady looks abashed first, then gestures for us to come in. She closes the door and ushers us to a room, which I assume to be the living room. Two empty cups are lying, I guess she just had some visitors. We sit on a peach - coloured sofa that is parallel to a table covered by a table linen of very elegant peach colour, having tassels at the corners with very intricate embroidery. Her house has the same colour and structure as

Cryde Myre's. She sits in front of us and stares at us as if waiting for us to proceed with whatever inquiry we have. John is the one to break the silence, "Thank you for sparing us your valuable time, ma'am. We just wanted to inquire about the case of one of your neighbor, Cryde Myre. Does that name ring a bell?" Her hands start shaking as her countenance changes to a look I can't quite decipher. She starts breathing hard, and my heart almost jumps out of my chest, god what is with old ladies and us giving attacks to them? John holds the same expression as I. Suddenly, a lady in a dark brown simple gown appears out of thin air, wearing an apron with a glass of water in hand and in haste feeds the old woman some kind of pill with water. It takes several moments for her to calm down as she regains her composure and breathes normally.

Thank God. “Are you okay?” I ask. “Yes, thank you. I have a problem with anxiety attacks.” The woman apparently, the maid hurries out of the room as I nod and start to hammer her with questions concerning the case. She almost has no answer to most of them, as she says that she hardly knew their family and met them only once or twice. “How would you describe their nature as per the few meetings you had with them?” She ponders for a few seconds and says, “They were the kind of people whom others wanted to be associated with. Down to earth, polite, helpful, caring, people like them are hard to find. It is a disgrace that they could not live long enough with their children whom they adorned.” Suddenly, the word children strikes me, and as if John has read my mind, he asks, “What do you mean by children? Didn’t they have just a boy?" She looks at us, amazed and doubtful. "Didn't you know they had a younger daughter, too?" It takes us a few moments to register the fact, what about the painting? There was only one child with them in the portrait. I think they had the baby after the photo was taken. "How younger was the girl than the boy they had?" "Not sure, but I guess around four to five years younger." Justifiable. "Do you have any idea who could have murdered them?"

"No," She says as a shadow of terror passes her face. We take it as a hint and take a leave.

Chapter - 15

We are driving back to the hotel while the faded sound of a song surrounds the environment. John breaks the silence by saying, "What should we do now, sir?" "Let's head back tomorrow. I think we are not going to find something else here." John nods in response. When we reach the hotel at around eight pm, we straight away go to have dinner and then head off to our rooms. The thoughts of the letter I found, the portrait, the connection between the two cases, the family suicide, and murder are too much at once. It is like I am getting lead, but I am not getting it all. The thoughts of the possibility of what could have happened are creating a whirlpool in my head. I crash onto my bed, and instantly, exhaustion-induced sleep engulfs me. The next day, I wake up and enter the tub filled with hot water. As I lie down in the tub, my whole body, knotted nerves and muscles relax. I ponder about the digit written in the letter if only the writer had written the name. The Pope's murder, his family's suicide and Cryde Myre’s murder case are connected, but how? The families were connected, that is for sure. Saunder Laurson’s words are a testimony. She said they were close before the two families met. What happened after they met? How did they meet? What relation did they share? Everything that is known about the two families is different, their background, their status, their lifestyle and everything was polar apart. I get out of the tub and wrap myself in a towel, and get dressed in casual trousers and a white shirt. I meet John in the lounge and proceed to make the payment, and after paying the tip, we make our way to the car. "Shall I drive?" I ask John. "As you wish, sir" I really need to give some rest to my brain. We enjoy the drive with light music. The route is the same, with accurately shaved bushes passing us and people moving on and busy in their lives. We pass several lights and are fortunate enough not to have come across any red light, which spoils all the rhythm of the driving. We reach New York in the afternoon, which is evident by the traffic. "Shall we stop anywhere to have a meal, sir?" "Why, you famished?" I ask. "No, sir, I thought maybe you were hungry so we could grab a bite." Just as John says this, I hear the growling of his stomach that could be heard from even a mile. His whole face turns crimson due to the mortification of being caught in his lie. I try hard to hide the smile threatening to break, and miserably fail. "I am quite famished, let's grab a bite," I say while the mocking tone makes its appearance in my voice. John looks at me like I've abashed him more, which I think I have. Since we're in New York, looking for restaurants is also not needed; there are several restaurants once we enter the main city. The traffic becomes heavier as we enter deep into New York. Small buildings start arising on the side of the roads, and the nature around us ceases as it gets replaced by the man - made creations. I stop the music and drive towards a subway. "Is a subway okay?" I ask while knowing the answer. "Okay, sir." It takes me around fifteen minutes to reach the subway. The parking lot is in front of the subway with adequate space meant to attract people, and by the looks of it, serving full justice to the motive it was made for. I park the car around the corner and turn it off as we proceed to make our way to the restaurant. "Let's order a..."

Chapter - 16

We part off after finishing our meals, John leaves in a cab while I head to my house after dropping the car at the police station. I reach home in the afternoon, while the silence greets me. After changing, I go to my room and drape the curtains to give a much-needed sleep. As I lie down, a sense of relief leaves me, home is home, and nothing can compare it in terms of comfort. I close my eyes and drift off to sleep, knowing that from tomorrow on, the same tiring routine will start and I might not get adequate sleep. I get up three hours later, still feeling the need to continue sleeping, but my stomach growls in contradiction. I lift off the blanket and stand up, opening the curtains. Outside is pitch black, only the lights of blue, red, and white colours indicating buildings and moving cars. As I watch the delightful view, a sudden thought comes to my mind. In one of these streets, which people adorn, there might be some gruesome and brutal crimes happening, which could probably shake us to our core and send shivers running down our bodies. Sometimes even the most beautiful sights might bear most atrocious acts. I think of all the crimes the same beautiful building, the walks of New York, have witnessed that are unknown to us. I go to the washroom to wash my face and brush my teeth. I feel fresh as I enter the kitchen to make myself a light dinner. I take out bread, cheese and spinach from the refrigerator and make myself a spinach sandwich. I might not be an excellent cook, but I can make good enough food that a person who does not have regular exquisite cuisines in a five - star hotel can like. I eat the sandwich like it might be my last one, devouring each bite. Suddenly, the doorbell rings, I look through the see - through hole and spot Randy. He is standing just enough distance away from the door that makes his face visible, his face is wearing an impatient expression. Out of nowhere, I am hit by the feeling of guilt for disappearing from the face of the earth without telling him anything. I open the door, preparing myself for the shit I would be getting from him. He strides inside and after closing the door, I usher him to the kitchen without a word. I grab my empty plate and the dirty utensil used to prepare the sandwich and put them in the sink. I turn to look at him, and he is looking at me without any expression while his arms are crossed over his chest. If this is the case, then… I grab the utensils and take my sweet time to wash and dry them, knowing I am playing with fire, but you can't blame a man for having a little fun after having a close to shitty and exhausting day. I glance at him while he still doesn't say anything, but his expressionless face is morphed into one of accusation. "Okay, fine, I should have informed." I'm close to snapping when I can't bear the weight of his gaze anymore. "You do not have any right to snap at me like this. I should be the one beating the shit out of you for not answering my calls and not deeming it necessary to tell you that you were off to someplace. Do you even think of me as your brother, or do you just say it, taking pity on me?" I should have known better than not to inform him about leaving to inquire about the case in Washington, his outburst and feelings of insecurity crack my heart into two. It is completely my fault. "I understand your emotions and promise you this won't happen again. I went for the investigation of a murder case to Washington, and trust me, if it wasn't as urgent as it was, I would have never forgotten to inform you." I say with utter sincerity in my voice, meaning every word. He looks at me with vulnerability in his eyes, and before giving it a second thought, I hug him. He hugs back after some hesitation. "Let's watch a movie, shall we, like old times?" I say to lift his mood, fully aware that it would consume the time that I wanted to rest in but knowing that sacrificing a few hours of sleep is nothing compared to what he deserves. He nods, and we switch on the television. The first channel that greets me is a news channel, a fair woman with black hair is holding a mike and almost yelling in it thanks to her enthusiasm. "The case of the murdered pope is still without any lead, or so we know, the appointed head officer is Sterlley Rampant and John..," I switch off the television while Randy again looks at me with hurt in his eyes due to hiding something from him. I don't tell him the details of the case as I'm not an authority to do so, but I always disclose the basic case I'm working on, and this is a huge case which I have gotten after a while. "So, wanna tell me something?" Fucking news.

Chapter - 17

The next day I get into my car and head towards my office ready to see the CCTV footage and DNA test results. I took me half an hour to convince Randy and explain the case. I was breaking a promise while making a promise. I park the car and make my way to my office. As I take a seat, I notice the footage and DNA results lying on the table. I open the DNA test, and the test group is AB+. It is not a big deal, as we do not have a suspect right now. I look at the footage of the outside of the church on the day of the murder on my computer in the office, and I see the priest that we had interrogated talking to a person who isn't visible with his back to the camera. He is wearing an expensive dress. People are pouring out from the door. Everything seems normal. I watched the whole video, finding nothing that could indicate a prospective suspect. I prepare a crisscross of threads on the whiteboard in my office linking each of the people that I have met in reference to the case. A knock disrupts my thoughts, and I see John peeping through the door. "John, come in," I say, glad to have some company. "Have you seen the results and the footage, sir?" He asks with a slight curiosity in his voice. "Yes, John. Why don't you have a look?" I say slightly while pushing the results towards him. He nods and proceeds to have a look. "Everything seems fine," he says when he has finished watching the footage. Suddenly, an officer enters the room and says, “Sir is calling you both to his room to give him a recap of the case investigation going on.” He leaves without waiting for a reply as we head towards Lauren’s office.

Chapter - 18

Lauren was as expected disgruntled but did not convey it by saying, not to say that the man has the most freaking expressive face in the world. John and I are sitting on my desk looking at the letter, photos and all the evidence we have accumulated so far. The footage does not provide any kind of special assistance; it would have been better if a camera had been installed inside the church. Then John's phone call rings, he picks up. "Okay, hmm, okay, thank you." After cutting his phone, he looks at me and says, "The reports came sir. Lauren did not die abnormally. Apparently, she already had several health problems that now or in the future could have been fatal for her." I nod, fully aware that we are thinking the same thing, why just before she was going to reveal something massive? I mean, I am not insensitive towards anyone's demise, but her words could have solved ninety per cent of the case. Now we are stuck with two freaking families linked, I don't know how, a few photos, a glove, interviews with several weird people and a fucking letter. Nothing is direct in this case; everything is twisted up. Maybe it's time we remember God.

Chapter - 19

I enter the church and are met by huge crowds of people. Out of the peripheral of my vision I see Stenhart, the priest whom we interrogated on our first day. “I don’t know whether to be sad or happy to see you here.” He says with a slight smile, tugging at the corner of his lips, filled with sorrow. So… maybe he has processed what has happened and can display sorrow like a human, unlike the first time. “I get it. The police are generally not the company that the people want to be associated with or to be visited by. Well, I just came to get a peace of mind." I say. "Yes, why not. Please have a seat, the prayer is just going to start." I take a seat, close my eyes and try to relax. The murmuring of people is audible in indistinct whispers. As the Lord's Prayer is started by the congregation, the whispers fade to silence. I revel in the feel of tranquillity I experience. Whatever it may be, I, being a non - religious person, still have to accept that when all doors close, the only door that is open to us is of God. He is our brightest star in a starless sky, hidden by clouds trying to overshadow his brightness and keep it from reaching us. Our talent should lie in overcoming our fear and gazing back at the dark sky with the hope of finding one trace of light. God is where we come from, God is where we go after death, and in the race called life, when we stumble, he is our helping rope. I lose myself in the serene and soothing environment adorned with the beautiful prayer, keeping my eyes closed. When I open my eyes after the prayer is done, I can clearly see through people and their need to come to church. Some come to thank God for some good, while some come to express sorrow. Some come to get his grace, while some come to listen to his tales. After a while, everyone is ready to head back to their houses after exchanging hugs and kisses. One person among the guests catches my eye. He is wearing high - end clothes and seems an emotional wreck. His eyes are red and are continuously flowing while his face is stained with streaks of tears. He seems to be in his forties or fifties, indicated by the little traces of wrinkles at the corners of his eyes. Father Stenhart approaches the man and talks to the man, probably offering condolences for the reason he is crying. The man talks to him and releases his pent - up emotions while the priest listens to him with a patience I thought was impossible to contain. The person, after a while, stops talking and glances back at me along with Father. It is at that moment that I realised I had been staring at them, completely oblivious that it might make them feel uncomfortable, lost in my own train of thought. I snap my neck with such suddenness in the opposite direction that I won't be surprised if I have a sprained neck afterwards. I am overcome by a wave of mortification as if a child has been caught cheating. I hear them approaching by the echo of their steps, clearly audible in the now almost empty church. You might tell me to dance like a fucking monkey in the middle of the church, and that wouldn't make me as mortified. "Officer, I want to introduce you to someone." I snap my neck sideways while standing up for God knows what conversation I would be encountering. I mean, I don't even know the man. "He is Carom and has recently shifted from Washington. It would be really helpful if you could be there for him if he needs any help in the future, which I think ought to happen in a city like NewYork. I wouldn't be asking you if I knew someone better than a cop who knows the city like the back of his hand." I am tempted to say no, but the look of despair in the red, swollen eyes of the man tears away at my humanity. "Yeah, why not. Nice to meet you, I am Officer Sterlley Rampant, and I would be happy to provide assistance whichever way I could." I say with a hint of sincerity in my voice.

Chapter - 20

I reach home in the afternoon and cook myself a delighted meal. I took Caroms number and talked to him for a brief moment. And by the brief talk I had with him, he seemed a reasonable person who came from a rather poor household and had shifted from Washington to Chicago. He did a job in the IT sector of a company, I did not bother asking, and he has been transferred here. After finishing my meal, and switched on the TV and put on Netflix to relieve my mind for a few hours by watching a delightful movie. It takes me twenty minutes to find a movie to entertain me for the evening. By the time I finish watching the movie, it is evening. The sky is changing its colour to a darker shade of blue, and the sun is disappearing behind the dense clouds. I switch off the TV, and suddenly I go to my room to have a good sleep. As I lay, my thoughts engulfed in a whole world of their own. The various questions floating around in my head make it hard for me to sleep while my body aches. After at least one hour of overthinking, I finally drift off to sleep. A sudden ringing startles me awake; it had been merely two hours since I slept. The name displayed on the screen is John, "Yes, John." "Sorry to disturb you, sir, but I have found something you should see on the footage." I had asked John to review a few weeks of the outside camera footage of the church, which could reveal any pattern of the person who committed this murder. It is evident that the person knew that the Pope would be alone that day till late. It has to be someone close to him, but he did not have any relatives, friends, and from what I have on him, he was not an amiable person. “Is it significant?” I ask while getting up from my bed and changing into appropriate clothes with the fastest pace I can. I am not wearing my uniform as it would take time, and I am just going to see the footage as it is already almost nine in a half hour. I am overcome with a wave of excitement and nervousness as I await the response. “Yes, sir, it is.” That is all I need to know before I spring into action, grab the car keys and march out the door.

Chapter - 21

I am ambivalent towards whatever evidence John has found, considering that all the evidence we have gathered has only pushed us into more intricate webs of mystery. The distance from my home to my office seems to have doubled overnight. As if I was not already impatient, the cars stopped as the red light approached. Great. The next minutes passed by in a haze of profanity. It takes me a moment to get out of my car after parking it and jogging towards my office. The office is almost empty, and the few people doing overtime pass me looks I don't want to recognise. I enter my office, where John is already seated. He looks up from the computer and passes me a look that makes me move towards my chair beside him, while anxious energy surrounds me. "I was looking into the footage of outside of the church, and I found this on the footage of the eleventh, that is one day after the murder." He then clicks on the video. The video displays the time on the corner that I take a note of in my mind. I can see the darkness enveloping the surrounding; not a single soul can be seen anywhere. Suddenly, a black car comes up on the side of the road and halts. It is a Honda Civic, the door of the car opens, and a man emerges from the driver's seat. He is wearing an expensive suit embellished with some kind of embroidery hard to neglect; his clothes scream affluence, but the car is just a normal one. I cannot see the man’s face due to the darkness and the cap he is wearing that conceals his face. The man gets out of the car and holds a packet in his hands, and walks across the door towards the church. Just as I think that he is going to enter the church, he stops walking and goes to the corner, takes out the gloves from his pocket, wears them and starts digging the soil near the corner vigorously. The packet is kept beside him. After one minute of relentless digging, he grabs the packet and puts it in the hole and starts putting mud on it. He stands up, jogs to his car, gets in and removes his gloves. And starts driving, I stop the footage and zoom in on the number plate, but the number is not visible. “The number plate is not visible, I already tried,” John utters. “Hm…, contact all the car rental stores in New York and inquire whether they lent a

Honda Civic to any person on the eleventh and twelfth," I say. "Why car rental stores? It is most probably his own car?" John asks. "Yes, it could be. But looking at his clothes, he is a wealthy man, but the car completely contradicts this. A man whose suit probably costs more than some people's monthly salary would think of it to be below him to buy anything less than an SUV or Mercedes. Affluent people are generally extravagant. Let's try our luck, otherwise we always know if this does not work, then the man has a black Honda Civic." John nods. "I'll be on it." I think of what the man buried, "Also, tomorrow we will see what has been buried on the corner of the church." I say hole standing up. Guess tomorrow is going to be an eventful day.

Chapter - 22

The next day I make my way to my office and the next moment John comes almost rattling the door. “Yes John, any information of the car?” I ask. “Yes, sir. I have talked to the owner of several car rental stores and have narrowed down two prime locations from where the car could have been taken. The other stores had either given the car to a lady, or the day did not match.” My guess was right then. Fortunately, the narrowed-down number is less than I expected. “So let’s go to the stores first, then we will go to the church to dig out whatever the hell is in that plastic." I speak. "Okay, sir," we make out the door, and John drives the car as he has the address to the place. The first store is quite massive; there are cars of every kind here and there. You name the model, they have it. The manager approaches us with a smile on his face, probably expecting us to rent a luxurious car, but as he comes closer, his smile fades as he registers our uniform. The person has a mix of black and white hair, which could be almost passed as grey and is slightly on the heavier side. "Hello, Mr Stark, I am John. Remember I called you and told you that I would be paying a visit soon to inquire regarding one of your cars?" The man slightly smiles, "Yes, I do remember. Please follow me, let's talk inside." We nod. He ushers us to one of the rooms inside his store. This room has pink painted walls, luxurious furniture with a set of black sofa against a wall. We take a seat, and the manager, Mr Stark, takes a seat beside us on the sofa beside ours. “Would you like to have something, a cold drink, coffee or anything?” he asks. “A glass of water would be sufficient, please, thank you.” I speak. “I’ll also take a glass of water, please.” John says. “Yeah, just a minute.” The man gets up from the sofa and goes out the door and the next minute returns with a person serving us water. “So, what would you like to know?” the man asks when seated on the sofa. “We wanted to inquire about the Honda Civics you had given on rent on the eleventh and twelfth. Any detail regarding the person could be really useful.” I speak. The man looks at me and John with a contemplating expression and after a few seconds says, “I’m sorry officers but would you mind explaining why I need to do so. Am I in trouble for some reason I'm not aware of. Was the car used for some crime of larceny or some other illegal activity." his face suddenly turns crimson due to terror as he most probably imagines the worst case scenario. "No, sir, nothing you need to be anxious about. We just needed the information of the person regarding a crime he could possibly be associated with. So, if you could comply with the needs to carry out the investigation, it would really be helpful." Mr Stark visibly relaxes, and his colour returns. "Yeah, sure, why not. We have the driver's license, phone number of the person and the name on our computer. If you want, I can show it to you," he says. "Yes, please." He takes the lead and guides us out the door, and that is when I notice that the place is actually majestic and contains several rooms. The place has walls, but in some places transparent glasses are fitted that somehow manage to make the place look more attractive. After passing several rooms, we finally enter a room that has a computer on a desk. A blond types away something on the computer at the speed of a metro. And trust me, that is not exaggerating. She seems young, maybe in her late or mid twenties. She stops as we approach her. "Medulla, would you mind taking out the details of the person who rented the Honda Civic car on eleventh and twelfth?" Mr Stark asks with an authoritative note in his voice. "Okay, sir. Just a moment, please." She again starts to type frantically, and after a few seconds, she has the details. Here, sir, these are the details; you can zoom in." Just as she turns the screen in our direction and I just as much as touch the keys to zoom in on the information, the information, barely visible due to its size, disappears as the screen goes blank. What the hell. "The information just vanished. Could you just bring it on again? I think I might have touched the wrong key," I say. John looks at me, thinking the same thing I am. The blonde whose name is apparently Medulla nods and turns the computer in her direction to do whatever technical shit people do. A few minutes pass as my anxiety eats away at the last remnants of my patience. Just as I am about to say something, she speaks up. "This is not a technical glitch sir; the information has been erased permanently by some anonymous person."

Chapter - 23

John and I are sitting on the sofa of the room we were first brought to. We asked the manager to arrange for the camera footage of the day the man came for the car, through his already instilled cameras at various places, even a glimpse of the person could serve as grievous evidence because if that person is not the fugitive then also he has a robust connection with the real culprit or could be an implicit in the murder. John has also asked them to check the tracker to get to know what route the car took on eleventh and twelfth to be sure that it is the same car, just in case. Otherwise, why would he risk his life for someone else? What we know of him, he is also a wealthy man. “Don’t you think, sir, that the person who could hack into a system with such a high level of security as theirs, could easily delete his camera footage?” John asks with a questioning look on his face. “Actually, I am pretty sure he has already done it, but in such a sensitive case, I do not want to leave any stone unturned.”, I say. The manager returns having a grim expression. “I have checked the tracker of the car, and as you said, it had taken the route to the church. But unfortunately, I could not gather the camera footage; some technical issue has occurred.” The manager says, while his face clearly gives away that he is still not able to process that someone could hack his system, and that is exactly what happened in the case of the footage as well. Well, I won't point that out because the man deserves no humiliation. "Yes. Okay. Could you give us the list of places the car had been taken to?" Mr Stark nods and again heads out the door, and in a while comes back. "You'll have to wait for a few hours. You can come in the evening and take the list because it may take some time." "I'll come in the evening." Stark nods. "Do you remember the description of the person, sir? Anything that could be used to identify the person?" John asks. "No, I don't remember anything worth telling. The person was wearing some rich clothes, that's all I remember. His face was covered by a mask. When he saw me looking at him, he said that his face was burned and that he didn't feel comfortable showing it." Okay, this is some new information. But it is obviously a lie the guy was telling to stop any more questioning. "Do you mind showing us where the car is? We have to take the fingerprints from its steering wheel." John asks. "I'm not sure that would be possible, we clean the cars when they arrive after being taken out by the people and use certain chemicals which to my knowledge, remove the fingerprints." The manager says with a sorry expression. "Are you sure? Yes, certainly. Well, then we'll take leave and thank you for the cooperation." John and I look at each other and head towards our car. Let's go to the church and find the glove that the person who most probably murdered the pope hid in the sand.

Chapter - 24

Sometimes I wonder how easy it would have been if there would have been cameras inside thc church as well. But again, the murderer could hack into it and delete the footage anytime, and the only reason that the camera outside the church remains protected is due to its out-of-the-ordinary and concealed location. Hell, even I might not have noticed it, had it not been the priest informing us. As we pass by the cars and trees beside ours, they seem to have indulged in a race with us. A person looking from the side of the road, however, would know the whole scene and the truth. Just the same way, I need to look at the case, probably from a new perspective. As I am pondering on the case, I am startled awake into the world of reality from my world of thoughts as John aggressively honks at a car. And by the looks people are directing our way, I am pretty sure there was no need for one. I look at John, and he seems to me anything but at ease. “Why do you look so agitated?” I ask. John, for a second, looks at me and then snaps his attention back to the road. “Nothing, sir. Just parents.” Okay. I get the hint. I won’t ask what happened, who did what, because it is not my business. I think John has the same thoughts, which are reflected in his polite dismissive words. After a few minutes, we get close to the church and a weird feeling I can’t get a grip on bounds me. We had already informed the priest not to allow anyone in the church today. As we reach, I notice that the entire area is silent and not a soul can be seen in the church or outside the church. The priest emerges from the opening doors. We head towards the church with gloves on our hands to dig in the area where we saw the footage of a man digging. "To what do I owe the visit officer?" the priest asks with a serious face. I think he did not like closing off the church for the day. "We have found a crucial piece of information which could prove to be the evidence we were looking for."

"Here at the church?" he asks with an astounded expression. Well, I don't blame him, even I had no clue that there could be anything related to the murder still at the church. Not exactly at the church, but outside, but one and all it's the same thing. "Yes, surprisingly. Outside the church, someplace here." John says while walking forward towards the area and kneeling before the place. I go towards him and kneel beside him while the priest follows me and looks at us with curiosity. The grass on the ground is trimmed and is uniform except for a patch in front of us. John starts to dig the area, and for a few moments, we find nothing. Just as I am about to give up and search in some other area, I see something. A plastic. John starts digging vigorously and pulls it out. A plastic inside which is a glove.

Chapter - 25

Just as we all are looking at the glove. John's phone rings, "Hello, yes, yes, okay. Sir the list has arrived. Let's go then, I will accompany you. We might find something vital that could provide a hint and point us in the right direction." We get up, and the priest looks at us as if we have grown two heads as he looks at us as if we are complete maniacs. I had almost forgotten that he was here. "Father, thank you for the corporation. Now we would take a leave," John says. "No problem, officer, may I open the church now?" He asks as if he were just waiting for us to leave so that he could open the church. Not at all concerned about the glove. “Yes, sir, you may now,” John says after filling the hole we had dug and holding the glove. “Send the glove to forensics and determine whether the glove is the other part of the glove we found at the house.” “Yes, sir,” we sit in the car and drive towards the rental shop. After some time, we reach the shop and see that the manager is already waiting for us there. We park the car and get off. The manager comes to hand us and hands us over the list. John immediately starts to scan the list. His eyes halt, and I immediately know that the church is on the list. He hands me the list, and I check the time, day and duration the car was there for; it completely matches the time the footage displayed. “Can we take the list?” John asks. “Sure, sir.”, he says without an ounce of hesitation. "We will get back to you if we need to. Thank you for your cooperation. We will take a leave." I say. He nods while displaying a half - smiling face. Just as we are turning, he speaks up. "Won't you like to come in and have a glass of refreshment. I… need to tell you something." We look at him. He looks uneasy, uncomfortable and unsure. "Would you mind?" He says while gesturing towards the office we went to previously. Without a question, we start to walk towards his office. As a policeman, I know that when a person speaks up to the police with uncertainty, they either did something wrong or did something wrong. We walk into the office and sit on the sofa while he sits in front of us. "So?" A server brings in two glasses of refreshment accompanied by some biscuits. After he leaves, the manager looks at us and says, "Officer I just remembered one thing that I wanted to tell, but I was afraid that you could suspect me if I suddenly come up with new information when you were here just this morning." At this point, it is hard to process that I should pity our reputation or the man in front of us. "Sir, you need to know that if we suspected you, you wouldn't be sitting here. You can trust us to trust you as long as we don't find any evidence indicating that you gave us the wrong evidence." John says in an unexpected way. The manager looks confused as fuck at first, but after a few moments gathers himself up, realising that it is a reassurance. "The man that you suspect had been here not just once but twice. The first time wearing a hoodie and the second time a mask, which obscured his face from me. He took the same car a few days ago and was wearing the same clothes. And a pendant. Stating the year nineteen ninety and twenty - eight June." I am still processing what I heard when John speaks in a low and hushed voice, only I can hear, "Sir, isn't this the day Cryde Myre and his family were murdered?"

Chapter - 26

" Do you have the records of the other day the car was taken? Yes, they are in the same list I gave you. I quickly take out the list from my pocket and scan it, and it states an address in Washington. Cryde Myres' house. The same one we visited. The same day we visited. What the hell. The two families are linked; that much is certain. But who is this person and why did he go to that house, how did he know its address, is he some relative of the deceased family? Nothing is clear. Visiting the house won't be of any help as we already went there that day and took anything of any relevance. The letter stating Big Brother. It is almost confirmed that the same person had written the letter. Does that mean that he was some distant relative of the family, because as far as I know, the family had a boy and a daughter and that both of whom were murdered along with the parents. "Could you do us a favour? We will call a forensic artist so you can describe the perpetrator. Just so we know what it looks like." The manager nods, "Sure." We stand up and leave. John drives the car, "John, make sure that the forensic artist arrives here the early. There is always risk involved with the eyewitnesses." I speak from experience; I have been in this profession for several years now and in most cases the witness is either bribed or killed. "Also, provide him with some security without his knowledge, just in case. We don't want him to panic, and with the amount of information he has provided, it won't be a surprise if the murderer tries to inflict the fear of terror in him or even kill him." I speak. "Yes, sir." Within a few minutes, we are back in my office. In front of me is a criss - cross of thread resembling a web. "We know that the murders are related. According to the time period, first, Cryde Myre and his family were murdered, then the Pope's family committed suicide. Cryde Myre's family was crazy rich, and in contrast, the Pope and his family were not in good condition. The old lady said that she was once their best friend. Did she have any family?" I ask. "She did have a son, but he severed all ties with her after the Pope's family committed suicide. People say that she got depressed and started neglecting her own child. She used to sit by the window all day long and remain listless. Even her child started having anger issues due to the atmosphere at the house. After one year, he left without a trace. Some people say that he was afraid that he might harm his own mother, and some say that he grew tired of all this. The locals also don't have a clue where he left. But there is another detail that I got to know, sir, the locals said that the son whose name was Bryan did not apparently have a liking for the Pope and his family because his mother always treated the Pope with motherly emotions and in pursuit of that neglected him." John says. "So if Bryan is alive, he could also be a possible suspect. He had anger issues, did not like the family and felt that his mother was drawn apart from him due to the Pope." I look at John and register his conflicted thoughts.

"Ask what you want to," I say to John. He looks hesitant at first, but eventually voices his thoughts, "The feeling of being neglected is not a good one, but can a person really kill to take vengeance against such a thing. Clearly, it was not the Pope's fault that he was loved more."

"John, the cases that I have seen have often included the jealousy factor as one of the triggers. As an adult also it is also hard to forget our childhood trauma. What effect could the murder of a family attached to him and his mother, and later the abject sadness his mother went into, have on a child's psychology and mentality? He also had, or if alive still has, anger issues, which could also be the driving force." I say, thinking of the way that I could derive some information about him if alive.

"If alive, he must have changed his name. If the car person we are suspecting is him, then he also should excel in technology, given that he deleted the details list from even the robust system of the rental store."

I speak. "The person, if alive, has probably become a monster; he did not come on his own mother's demise."

Chapter - 27

"Sir I did some research as to why the church was built in New York when Cryde Myre was living in Washington with his family. I found the contact of the person who, at that time, was investigating the case. He has retired now, but knew the reason. He told me that Cryde Myre and his wife had a love marriage, and the first time they met was in New York. Apparently, not only he but also his wife was a religious person. So, to thank god for everything, later on, when they became affluent, they thought there could not be any place better than New York to build a church, where it all started." I listen to everything John says and try to read between the lines, but nothing doesn't sound a bit suspicious. "He also did not have any enmity with anyone. Why would anyone not like a person who, even after his death, is praised by people for his community service and kind nature?" Who could have murdered them? What reason, if only I could find the person responsible. But I'm not even sure that he/she is alive. "Jealousy." I gaze at John as a child in the first grade, waiting for the teacher to teach him for the first time. "Sir, didn't you say that jealousy is mostly the driving case. Anyone could be overpowered by the feeling of jealousy. It could be due to the relationship between brother and sister, girlfriend and boyfriend or friends longing for attention, love or care of a mother." I look at him skeptically. "So, you mean that it could be Saunders Laurson's son who could have murdered them out of jealousy. But he must have been only a teenager back then." Just as I say this, I know that it is not a reason that could be used to excuse. Many serial killers were children; this is still a teenager we are talking about. John passes me a weird look, and I have no intention of acknowledging. "So, he could have killed the family, compelled them to commit suicide or murdered them and then made it seem like a suicide. And maybe he felt guilty afterwards and left the place. An individual who apparently ran from home because he thought he could hurt his own mother, what is the chance that he could not kill another family?" I look at John and ask him, "Could we contact the same person you talked to, to inquire regarding the child. He must know something. He handled the case of Cryde Myre, so he must have some knowledge regarding both families as they are connected." John nods and goes away to make the call. He returns after a full five minutes, "He is ready, sir, but he is only willing to talk today as he is in this city for some work and would be heading back tomorrow. He told me the address that he would be reaching in one hour. The Denar Coffee shop." I nod, and we make our way to our car as the address John just said is almost forty - minute drive, excluding traffic. We drive in silence for a few minutes, and as it starts to get awkward, I switch on the music, and suddenly a song makes its way and cracks the wall of awkwardness. After a relentless drive of forty minutes, we reach our destination. I park the car, and we make our way to the side table in the coffee shop and take a seat. The shop is well furnished and has weirdly accurate, decorated embroidery at the ends of the tablecloth. The shop is not filled to the brim but is rather empty, I think this is the reason he chose this place so that we could have some privacy. We sit in silence for a few minutes and a waitress approaches us and asks in a gentle voice, "What would you like to have sir?"

"Actually, we were waiting for someone, so we will order with them," John says. He waitress nods and, with a slight smile, turns back and goes. Even if I don't want anything, it is not ideal to come to a coffee shop to chat and not order anything. I'll just have a damn normal coffee. From the peripheral of my vision, I spot a man, I look at him, and he seems to be in his mid - sixties. This is definitely him. Finally, we are going to get some answers that are not going to tangle our minds more.

Chapter - 28

He straightaway comes to our table as if we three have been best friends since old times. He is wearing brown coloured shirt with normal jeans and black boots. It is then that I realise John has been waving at him. He sits down on the chair, and we all form a circle around the table. "Hello, sir, I am Sterlley Rampant. Thank you for sparing us time." He casually takes my hand, and I feel his firm grip. I guess he is not as weak as he looks. "Not a problem, I was anyway here for a few days. And I guess we have already talked, John.

Right." He says, leaving my hand and turning his attention towards John. "Yes, sir." We sit in silence for two to three seconds, and just as I am about to ask the questions we are here for, the waitress we saw earlier comes back and asks us in the same enthusiastic voice of hers. "Sir, would you like to order something?" I want to straightaway say no, but it is not her fault; it is her job. I pick up the menu on the table and pretend to look at the different flavours available for half a minute, and then order a normal coffee as decided earlier. John orders a drink I think I can't even name properly, and the man whose name I now realise I don't know, doesn't order anything. The waitress scribbles down the orders and goes off in the direction of the counter. "Shall we proceed without delaying now," I ask with a genuine smile. The retired officer nods, and I don't think twice before shooting my questions. "You must know of Saunder Laurson. I would be grateful if you could tell me about her son. Anything minute to minute." I say. "Her son was not different from other kids, or so I thought in the beginning. He, like other children, had a problem with his mother, but over time, his behaviour started to turn into rage. This rage was due to neglect from his mother, even when he thought that he would get love and support from her after their demise, but he was wrong, she went into depression and barely talked four to five sentences in a day. It was kind of weird to see someone this depressed over their friend's demise, but then I came to know that the pope's mother had been best friends with her all her childhood, and they were sisters more than friends. As far as I can tell of the kid is that he was a very unpredictable one. Sometimes very cooperative, other times very moody." I nod, "Do you know how both families knew each other?" I feel my anxiety level up while asking this question, as this might provide an answer to a lot of questions. "Yes. As you might know that, Cryde Myre was not an affluent person always. At that time, he met the Pope's parents somewhere, and they became quite good friends, and even the Pope had very frequent visits to their place. He was deeply attached to Cryde Myres' son, and cvcn thc son rcgardcd him as his cldcr brothcr. Although Myre was not rich but he was still notched above the Pope's family's financial condition. But since he was a very down - to - earth person, all this hardly mattered to him. He started his own business with the help of the Pope's father, whose name apparently was Jack Lopez and later on, his business grew to such an extent that any amount of money hardly mattered to him. But the condition of Jack remained the same because he was merely there in the beginning for a few months, and later on, he left the business because he did not believe in it and was in despair regarding it. After he left, Myre alone carried the business for years, and after facing a lot of hardships, he accomplished, which is evident from the reputation he has even now and the money. Obviously, there was regret in Jack to leave the business they both started together with both their ideas, but this regret never came between their sweet as sugar friendship." We ask him a few other questions that could help us do a scrupulous investigation, and after a few minutes, thank him for meeting us and almost bid our goodbyes as I stop and call out his name, "I am sorry, but could you tell me by what name Myre's son used to call the Pope. I mean, if he respected him that much, he must not have used to call him by his name, right?" He shoots a faint smile towards me, "He used to call him big brother."

Chapter - 29

John and I are sitting at my office and evaluating each and every aspect. "So, we know that they started a business together but it was only carried on by Myre." The most mind dazzling thing in my mind is the letter we found in Myres mansion, which was from according to the letter someone who called him big brother. But that could be anyone, Cryde Myres' son could not have written the letter because he is dead. He is, right? Of course, his body was found. Then, only one option is available; someone is fucking with our heads. I take out the letter and look at the number. 45114121516526. I try to twist the number whatever way I can to derive it to Big Brother. It doesn't work. I even write the alphabet according to the numbers, but that also doesn't work. Then I realise that I forgot to check the main name 4-D,5-E,1-A,14-N,12-L,15-O,16-P,5-E,26-Z. This is it. DEAN LOPEZ. The letter was really for him. We just have to find out who wrote it. Maybe it is Bryan. We are aware that the person has a pendant. I take out the picture that I had received, made according to the provided descriptions by the manager. It has the year nineteen ninety and twenty-eight June written on it. The day the Myres family was murdered. It is just then that I receive a call from an unknown number. "Hello, who is this?" I ask. "Hello officer, Carom this side. I am really sorry to interrupt you, but I really needed some assistance. I would really not have disturbed you, but I really don't know anyone here. Could you spare me some time?" Oh shit, it was supposed to be me calling him and inquiring, but in the midst of the case, I completely forgot. "Oh, yes, hi, sure" What the hell am I saying? "Surely, I would help you. By the way, how is New York treating you?" I try to sound as little impertinent as possible, which is completely in contrast to my actions, considering I did not even call the guy once. "It is treating me fine till now and hopefully will in the future also." He speaks. "Nice. Tomorrow, do you think it's fine then?" I ask, while reciting several profanities, my direction when I remember my Sunday is gone. "Goes well with me."

Chapter - 30

I keep my phone down and so does John. "Sir, you were right. A person had visited last night." I had asked John to appoint certain officials to keep a check on Saunder Laurson's house, just in case someone visited. "The cameras installed there cannot be used to identify the person, though, as it was quite dark. But certainly, it must be him. Her son." I have no doubts pertaining to this. It makes more sense now that he would visit at night, so no one recognises him. Even if his name and looks have changed, there can't be much difference. "Did he have any vehicle he came by? Has any person seen him? Anything of evidence?" I ask with bare desperation dripping off my voice. "No, sir. You can have a look if you want, but the officials spotted nothing of evidence. The only thing we can be sure of is that her son is alive and came to visit. If it was at all, it was someone else he would have surely not come at night, hiding from people." I nod. Now we just have to find her son. "I still want you to interrogate each person living there close by. Anyone could have seen him. I don't want to take a chance." John nods. I take a mental note of all the evidence we have gathered so far. We are very close; we just have to find this person, which should not be that hard. Even if one person saw him, then game over. We can easily trace him. After around two hours of deep thinking and watching the footage of the house which was installed, we head off to our homes. The footage barely contains anything; the face of the person is not visible because it is dark, he is wearing a full black hoodie and considering only his back is to the camera. His standing position has to be arbitrary because if he really knew of the camera, why would he even come within its sight? And the weird thing is that he is merely standing there, no sobbing, no crying, just standing still as a rock. Maybe he is just an emotionless jerk, just there to look at the place that destroyed his childhood rather than remembering his mother. I reach home and head off to my bedroom. I don't have the power to even cook anything now; it has been an exhausting day. We are so close to finding the culprit. In just a few days, I would have a hold on him. I keep thinking for a few minutes that I don't realise when darkness prevails by overshadowing the light.

Chapter - 31

I wake up the next day in a free mode, fully intending to enjoy my Sunday keeping aside all my thoughts of the case, overcrowding my mind. I cook my breakfast and make myself a decent meal of bread and egg with a cup of coffee. Just as I am about to go off to taking a bath, a message pops up on my phone. I open the message. It is from Carom. Oh shit. Carom. I had to assist him today. Great, first I forgot to ask him if he needs my help, and now I forgot to contact him even after he has approached me to help him. The message is asking me the time and sending me the address. I respond and go to the washroom and within three to four minutes take a bath, put on casual's head to the address I have received. The drive is smooth, and as I reach closer and closer to the address, the scenery keeps getting better and expensive. Suddenly, the ringing of my phone startles me. I pick up the call and see that it's of Carom. I was just about to call him anyways. "Hello Carom, I am almost there. Where are you?" I ask. "I am standing in front of my house. Can you see, I think I can see you." Just as he says this, I am able to see a figure waving in the front at the corner. I pull up the car in the parking lot and get off. As soon as I get off, I see a truck parked on the side containing furniture, clothes and god knows what. "Sorry to disturb you, officer, but I just thought that setting up my home on my own would be better. But still, I needed some assistance." He speaks. "I have absolutely no problem. Shall we go in?" I ask. He nods and ushers me in. The house is rather big, not big enough to be called a mansion, but also not small. It is mostly empty inside the ring. He has not started unpacking any of his stuff. It is then that I realise that he has a small bandage on his forehead. I think of inquiring him about it, but decide otherwise. "Do you know when I first met the priest, he narrated a story of a boy whose family was killed by a person whom they trusted the most. The boy who killed did it for money, as the family was very rich. And the company that they owned was started by his parents as well as them. But due to some issues, they had to leave the company. After whose success, the boy held grudges. He just narrated this story to me and told me I should never trust anyone blindly in my life. At that moment, he seemed to lose." "Maybe he remembered an incident that happened to him. Should we get started then?" I ask. He nods and goes to a room and brings out a box. "This has clothes, just take them out and keep them in the room's cupboard." I nod. I take the box to the room he instructed me to and notice a huge black cupboard open. I open the box and keep the clothes in the cupboard, I must say he has quite a massive collection of them. As I am digging through the clothes, I look at a piece that is astonishingly beautiful with work that shows off its hard work. Just as I am on the last piece of cloth, I see a piece of paper. I pick it up and notice that it is a prescription of a doctor. It has the address of the doctor whose description is provided. I have no business looking at someone's medical condition, but I do it out of curiosity, setting aside my moral qualms. It names a condition which seems not only complicated in nature but also in spelling. Intermittent Explosive Disorder. What the hell is that? "Are you done with the cupboard?" Carom's sudden voice tears through my thinking, and I keep back the paper in haste. I pile up the clothes; however, I think they are in proportion and keep them in the cupboard. "Yes, done."

Chapter - 32

The next day I meet John at the office. "We cannot trace him, his has most probably changed his name and identity," I say. "Do we go there again to see whether anyone saw him or not? No one would have seen him, as it was late at night." Just as I am going to say something, I see a bruised Carom passing by the corridor. What the hell. I get up from my seat with the speed of lightning and dash off towards him along with John, following me close behind. "What happened officer," I ask the officer holding him. Nothing, a fight that could have escalated really fast. The officer notices my confusion and elucidates that he was the one who started the fight. I look at Carom, and that is when I notice that he is looking at me with a look I can't place. Just as I am going to ask him what happened, I receive a call. It's from an unknown number. I pick it up "Hello, officer. I have recalled some information you might want to receive." As I hear the voice, I know who is speaking. It is the lady whom we interviewed in the posh neighbourhood. I am just going to ask who told her my phone number, as I recall I gave it to her. "Do you want to meet?" I ask. "I am comfortable speaking on the phone if that is okay," She responds. "That is fine. Just give me a minute." I turn in the other direction and head towards my office, beckoning John to follow the suit. I enter my office and close the door after John enters. I put the phone on speaker. "Yes ma'am, what is it that you want to tell." I say. "I wanted to tell you that there was another family who became very close to them. A poor family that had a boy whose name I am forgetting. But he was sometimes known to have had anger outbursts. He was also arrested for a certain days for getting into a fight with a bunch of boys. He threw a stone at one boy, and the boy survived but had to be in the hospital." I take notice of each word she is saying. So if the person was arrested, his data must be stored somewhere in the records. AND CAN BE EXTRACTED. "That is all I wanted to tell." She says with a tone. "Thank you, ma'am, for taking the initiative to give a call and informing," I say while all the possible outcomes of the new information pass through my mind. "No problem." I keep the phone down and look at John. "It's him, isn't it?" I keep on looking at him, and we both pass on looks to each other that only we know what mean.

Chapter - 33

After all the formalities are done with Carom, I take him back to his place. Its not like he asked me but I was just leaving and he was booking a taxi and it all just did not sit well if I went off without offering a ride. As we are sitting in the car, there is utter silence. It's Carom who breaks the thick awkwardness by speaking. “It’s not what you think, okay. It's just that I have issues. Like real issues of anger. I even go to a doctor for it. It is due to my fucked - up childhood.” I keep on driving and say, “It’s okay, you don’t have to explain. Is it anything serious? This problem of yours." I just want to keep the conversation going because I cannot tolerate the silence once more. We keep on talking about various issues, and I am grateful when we reach his place. He gets out of the car and offers to come inside, I almost decline but say yes as my day is almost done, and I think he could use some company. As we go inside, I notice that he has not unpacked anything much. Everything is still lying in the boxes, and there are wrappers of plastic, tapes, and scissors lying from place to place. He gives me some water. "I am sorry for the mess. Actually, I did not have much time to unpack due to work," he says, looking even more embarrassed than before. "No, not a problem. Actually, now that is am here, shall I help you unpack?" I ask. "No, I really don't want to intrude on your time again." He speaks. "You won't be intruding. I want to help. And I think you need some help." He looks doubtful and hesitant at first, but agrees. I go to the same room I went to the one day I came and assisted. The room looks almost ready with the curtains adorning the windows. I still open the cupboard to see whether everything is set and nothing needs to be unpacked. The cupboard is filled with clothes. I think he has done this room first. Just as I am going to close the cupboard, I see an embroidered suit. It is strikingly captivating and expensive. Just as I try to dismiss the thought, I am hit by a sudden realisation. Suddenly, I feel my heart beating at a very high rate. Without thinking, I scan the clothes. I grab my phone and take a picture of the slip I found the first day. Knowing what I am doing is quite vague, I close the cupboard, keeping everything in place and run towards the exit door. Carom notices me running and shouts, "What happened? Everything okay?” “Yup, everything is okay. Just got an urgent call from the police station.” He says something, but I cannot hear it due to the constant thumping of my heart and me going distant with each passing step. If what I am thinking is true, then what the hell. I get in my car and start driving towards the address on the slip. It is not that far away, just a few minutes' drive. As I reach, I see a building with parking in the front. Thankfully, there is still a parking lot left. I park my car and almost start running towards the lift, I see just as I enter the building. I stop in my tracks when I hear a delicate but stern voice calling my name, “Sir, you need to register first if someone has called you.” I turn towards her, and in haste, I show her my police ID card. Before she can say anything, I run towards the lift and click on the floor where the doctor is. If only I know what condition he has. What I am thinking is quite vague, but there is a possibility. I reach the floor and see the name of the doctor written outside one door. This floor only has two rooms opposite each other. I go inside and see people sitting on a sofa, waiting for their turn. I see a girl jotting down something on her tablet. She seems to be in her mid - twenties. Without a second thought, I approach her, "I need to see the doctor." She looks straight up and passes me an impatient expression.

"Everyone here is to see the doctor, sir. I would request you to wait till the time of your appointment. Could I get your name, please?" She asks, scanning her list. "I don't have an appointment. It's urgent." I say, taking out my ID and showing it to her. She opens her mouth to say something, but doesn't say anything. I take that as a clue to go to the room. I enter the room and see the doctor sitting on a chair. "Yes, how can I help you?" He says while telling me to sit down. He thinks that I am one of his other patients. "I am here from the police station. I need you to share the details of a patient's problem. Actually, he is my friend, and I am worried about his condition. He is not feeling well, so he asked me to come here and talk to you." The doctor looks at me like he could not comprehend what I said. "I am sorry, I don't understand. What patient are you talking about?" "Carom. He was just arrested, and I am in the police. He just told me about his condition, so I needed you to tell me how his issue can really be controlled. He is running out of control. Well, here is the slip he gave me to come here. Just in case you need proof." I show him the slip. He takes a look. "Okay, his condition is due to his childhood…"

Chapter - 34

After I have had a word with the doctor, I am in a shock. Suddenly, I see John approaching. He gets out of the car and approaches me. Are you sure, sir, that what you are thinking could be true? “Even I know it sounds a bit weird and unplausible, but these kinds of cases are generally the most unpredictable. And all the evidences that match, so let’s see.” He nods. John suddenly gets a call. He looks at me, and I look at him. We pass on a conversation, “Pick it up.” John picks it up and nods. After a minute or two after disconnecting, he says, "It has matched." Shit. Is this really happening? I mean, till the time we were not sure, I knew that there was a plausibility that my interpretation was wrong. But now, it is all clear. "He was already in front of me all this time. Explains the deletion of the data from the computer of the rental store, as he told me he works at an IT company or something related to computers. He has the anger issues that everyone mentioned. Now, his prints have matched. I knew we would have his records if he was arrested in the past as well. He also came to the church and was crying. I did not know the reason just till now, but now I do. Because his mother died a few days ago. His mother. Saunder Laurson."

Chapter - 35

I come out of the office, after explaining what we found, the clues, everything. I did not go to arrest Carom as a suspect; I don't know. Something doesn't add up. Something doesn't seem right. Maybe it's me overthinking. Just as I am immersed in my thought, I hear a voice. Carom. I quickly go to the door and see John bringing John. "You're making a mistake. You've got to be kidding me. You. What the hell is wrong with you? You have got to be kidding me. Arresting me for a murder." John takes him before he can say anything more. I feel guilty for I don't know what. After a while, I decide to go to the church. John accompanies me. We both sit inside for a while. When the priest emerges, I stand up and tell John to be seated. I notice that he is holding a basket with several photos and flowers. "Good morning, father. I just wanted to tell you we have found a possible suspect." He looks interested at first. "Carom." I try to register his expressions, but he regains his composure. "How is this possible, I mean…" "Even though we are not sure but he is a possible suspect. The priest nods. I will just be back after keeping this basket. I nod. As he turns, something clinks against the floor. Just as I am about to call his name, I see something shining. It is a pendant with a specific year written on it. And the other is a photo of… Cryde Myre and his family. Do you know when I first met the priest, he narrated a story of a boy whose family was killed by a person whom they trusted the most. The boy who killed did it for money, as the family was very rich. And the company that they owned was started by his parents as well as them. But due to some issues, they had to leave the company. After whose success, the boy held grudges. He just narrated this story to me and told me I should never trust anyone blindly in my life. At that moment he seemed to lose.

The priest has a minor mark on his hand, which is negligible if not paid attention to.

Their faces are not displaying any emotion, but I can point to a flicker of pain latched onto the nun's face, which is almost negligible if you don't pay any special attention to it, while the priest's face is hard to comprehend.

Two empty cups are lying, I guess she just had some visitors.

I look at the priest. He is holding an embroidered…. shit. The rich old lady was also with him; it was not a matter of great concern to get Carom allocated here for her. But how is this murder linked to the Myre family?

The body of the boy was never found.

Is he the same boy? The son of the Cryde family. He wrote brother in the letter. Does it mean the pope was… Shit. According to the letter, it was the pope who killed his family. Betrayal means that only in the letter. It means the family that committed suicide was the Pope's family. Maybe they knew about the crime committed by the pope. The lady. She gave me a call deliberately to tell me about his problem just to frame him indirectly. It was all planned. He was always watching. What we found, what we planned, was always according to him. It was what he wanted us to see. I look at him. He is staring at me. And smiling.